For my mom, Penny.

— K. B.

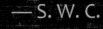

For my guides, who have helped me face fears
and turn them into discoveries.

— S. W. C.

Published in 2017 by Eerdmans Books for Young Readers,
an imprint of Wm. B. Eerdmans Publishing Co.
2140 Oak Industrial Dr. NE, Grand Rapids, Michigan 49505
www.eerdmans.com/youngreaders

Text © 2017 Katy Beebe • Illustrations © 2017 Sally Wern Comport

17 18 19 20 21 22 23   9 8 7 6 5 4 3 2 1

Manufactured in Malaysia

Library of Congress Cataloging-in-Publication Data

Names: Beebe, Katy, author. | Comport, Sally Wern, illustrator.
Title: Nile crossing / written by Katy Beebe ; illustrated by Sally Wern
  Comport.
Description: Grand Rapids, MI : Eerdmans Books for Young Readers, 2017. |
  Summary: "Khepri, who lives in ancient Egypt, begins to feel nervous as he
  and his father travel to Thebes for Khepri's first day of scribe school"–
  Provided by publisher.
Identifiers: LCCN 2016057818 | ISBN 9780802854254 (hardback)
Subjects: | CYAC: First day of school–Fiction. | Anxiety–Fiction. |
  Egypt–History–To 332 B.C.–Fiction. | BISAC: JUVENILE FICTION / School &
  Education.
Classification: LCC PZ7.B3823 Nil 2017 | DDC [E]–dc23 LC record available at
  https://lccn.loc.gov/2016057818

The illustrations were created digitally and with pastels and acrylic paint.

NILE CROSSING

Written by

Katy Beebe

Illustrated by

Sally Wern Comport

Eerdmans Books for Young Readers

Grand Rapids, Michigan

We wake in the still darkness

of a day unlike all others.

I roll up my mat, and my heart

swoops like a falcon in this new day,

the first day of school.

In the flickering glow of the lamp,

Mother knots an amulet around my wrist.

To keep me safe, she says with a kiss.

It is a scarab, like my name, Khepri.

She tucks three honey cakes into my belt.

A treat for later.

My little sisters are still asleep as we leave.

I shut the door softly.

As Father and I step into the deserted
street and turn down the old road,
my feet are heavy, but my head is light.

My Lord Thoth, the moon, glosses my father's
shadow silver in the darkness,
and above us the quiet seems to shine down
from the stars.

Today, on this day alone, we carry no nets,
and my cat, slinking behind us in the shadows,
will be disappointed.

The Nile welcomes us long before we reach it,

like a friend running to meet us.

It greets us with the whisper of reeds,

the lap of water at the riverbank,

the muttering of geese as they

mumble in their sleep.

I walk close beside my father.

He puts a reassuring hand on my shoulder,

and the words we do not say

fill the hush of dawn.

We reach my father's boat, and I sit at my
usual place, among the sweet smell of mud
and water and fish and rope.
But today my hands are empty.
As Father pushes us off
and the great river takes us up,
the Nile seems as wide as the sky,
with just the two of us sailing
in its gathering light.

Behind me, Father begins to sing our usual paddling song,
deep and low.
I start to sing too,
and our voices travel side by side over the still river:
My Lord Crocodile Sobek and my Lady Hippo Taueret
will not trouble us today.
Our hooks will be sharp, our nets heavy, our family full.
A fisherman's life is the best life of all.
Father and I fall silent, thinking the same thoughts.

Then, almost at once, the bright bead of the sun rises in the east

and drops light like honey into the river patterned by my father's pole.

I know without Father telling me that it is

my Lord Sun, the scarab Khepri, my namesake,

making his journey as well.

As he begins to sail his barge across the sky,

I break a honey cake in half.

The sweetness crumbles on my tongue,

and I try to be brave.

Our crossing is too long and too short,

and when we step into the cool mud on the other side,

I want to stay and to go,

to enter the town, thick with people and excitement,

and to return to our old, quiet river, and home.

But my father stands on the bank waiting,

and I put my hand in his,

and we cross through the marsh

and we cross through the fields

and we enter the great gate of Thebes.

Father knows right where to go.

Soon we stand before a courtyard,

but we do not go in.

In the street beside us

men pass, dressed in the brightest linen.

The city around us is waking up,

and my Lord Khepri's barge is climbing higher.

It is almost time.

My father presses a box into my hand.

It is a fine, long case filled with reeds,

but these reeds are not for fishing.

These reeds are pens for writing.

And today, on this day unlike all others,

instead of trailing them in green river water,

I will dip them, the tools of a scribe,

in ink of black and red,

the colors of the Nile mud and the desert.

I look at my father
standing tall and brave in the busy street,
and he looks at me
standing tall and brave looking at him.
The words we do not say
make the noise of the city silent.

Then my father clasps me to himself
and lets me go
and turns and makes his way
down the crowded street,
back to the river,
alone.

As I stand outside
the courtyard,
I hear the other boys
talking and laughing inside.
My new pen case
is strange in my hand.
Already I miss the feel
of the net and the
weight of a good catch.

I stand outside the courtyard, about to go in,

and I wonder if it is always this way

on the first day of school.

And yet, my mother's amulet is tight around my wrist.

My father's pen case is smooth in my fingers.

My Lord Khepri's favor is warm on my shoulders,

and I am not alone.

WRITING IN ANCIENT EGYPT

After Khepri gathers his courage to enter the school, he finds that his classroom is just an open-air courtyard. The teacher invites him to take his place, cross-legged, on the dusty ground next to the other boys. While the teacher recites a prayer to Thoth, the ibis-headed god of writing and wisdom, one of Khepri's classmates pulls out his schoolbook. It isn't the sort of book we think of, but a hardened piece of clay, an *ostracon*, with words written on it. Papyrus, the paper made out of strips cut from the papyrus plant that grows by the Nile, is used only for the most important writings, because it is expensive and takes so long to make. Even the words are different from the ones you may be used to. Instead of letters making up sounds that make up words, Egyptians in Khepri's time use small pictures, or hieroglyphs, that each represent one syllable or a whole word. To Khepri's surprise, the boy snaps the *ostracon* in two and shares one of the pieces with him. *New friends, not just new tools, are also important on the first day of school*, thinks Khepri. "Thanks," he says.

To write the name of the god Thoth, Khepri slides the cover off his wooden pen case and takes one of the pens from the slot underneath. The pens are made from slender reeds that also grow on the banks of the Nile, and they have a comforting, familiar smell for him. Then, while the teacher is busy helping a few of the older students, Khepri's friend shows him how to take his knife

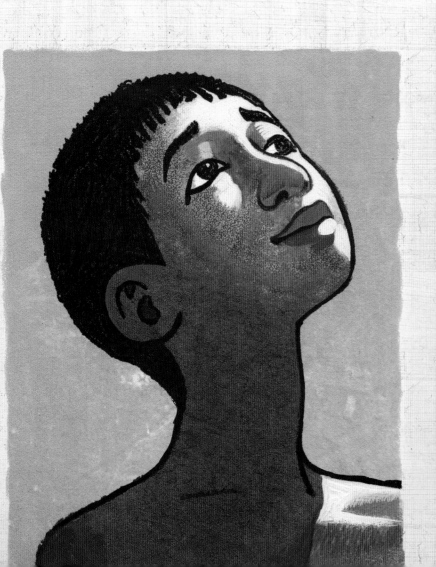

and cut the end of the pen, slightly crushing the tip to make it softer. Next, he dips the tip into water and shows Khepri how to brush the pen across one of the cakes of ink at the end of his pen case. The dark black ink is made by mixing soot with water and a sticky gum from the acacia tree. The red ink, made of a pigment called ochre, or iron oxide, is used for titles or headings—where we would use capital or bold letters. Finally, Khepri's friend helps him draw an ibis—the sacred bird that forms the first sign of the god's name. Khepri slowly traces its long curved beak, S-shaped neck, wings folded over an oblong body, and the two thin legs, onto the hard clay. "Good," the boy says with a grin. "Now you just have to learn about seven hundred more signs, how they go together in a thousand different ways, and all the sacred texts. Not a bad start, as the serpent said when he swallowed the toe of the hippopotamus."

"Thoth"

SCHOOL IN ANCIENT EGYPT

Khepri was not an actual person, but he could have been. His story is set in the Egyptian New Kingdom (c. 1550–1070 BCE), when the famous pyramids at Giza were already more than a thousand years old. The first sections of the Great Wall of China wouldn't be built for another five hundred years after Khepri was born, and the United States was still three thousand years in the future.

Most Egyptian children who went to school during this time were the sons of rich government officials, not fishermen. Students learned reading, writing, and arithmetic, and trained for jobs in the government as scribes, courtiers, administrators, priests, and even artists. Women did not work in these professions, and so most young girls probably did not get a formal education.

However, a few tantalizing bits of evidence suggest that a least a few boys from ordinary families, as well as some girls, did learn to read and write. In *The Satire of the Trades*, which was written at least two hundred years before Khepri's time, a father describes placing his son in a school with children of parents of far higher status than himself. And letters from regular working people, dating from Khepri's own era, have been found in a village near Thebes. Some of these letters were written to or by women, and so we can guess that at least a few non-royal women could read and write in the New Kingdom.

FURTHER READING

Booth, Charlotte. *An Illustrated Introduction to Ancient Egypt*. Stroud, UK: Amberley Publishing, 2014.

Green, Roger Lancelyn. *Tales of Ancient Egypt*. New York: Puffin, 2013.

McDonald, Angela. *Write Your Own Egyptian Hieroglyphs*. Berkeley and Los Angeles: University of California Press, 2007.

McGraw, Eloise Jarvis. *The Golden Goblet*. New York: Puffin, 1986.

McGraw, Eloise Jarvis. *Mara, Daughter of the Nile*. New York: Puffin, 1985.

Mertz, Barbara. *Red Land, Black Land: Daily Life in Ancient Egypt, 2nd Edition*. New York: William Morrow, 2009.

Weitzman, David L. *Pharaoh's Boat*. Boston: Houghton Mifflin Harcourt, 2009.

AUTHOR'S NOTE

I was taken to the Egyptian gallery of the Nelson-Atkins Museum of Art in Kansas City before I could even walk. On family road trips, instead of playing "I Spy," my mom (a third-grade teacher and amateur Egyptologist) would read to us from her adult, nonfiction books on ancient Egypt. I distinctly remember driving across the Kansas plains, listening to *Red Land, Black Land* by Barbara Mertz, the sky as bright a blue as I imagined it would be over the Nile. Between the ages of ten and fourteen, I also read Eloise Jarvis McGraw's *The Golden Goblet* about forty million times. The colors and the feel of Egypt in her novel were a great inspiration to me and shaped much of my sense of that era.

I've also had the luck to live in two cities with wonderful museum collections. I haunted the Metropolitan Museum of Art's Egyptian galleries when I worked in New York, and while studying in Oxford, England, I popped in to the Ashmolean's Sackler Gallery of Egyptian Antiquities any time I had a spare moment. There's a pen case in the Ashmolean, from the Middle Kingdom burial of Neteruhotep, that I imagine must be very much like the one given to Khepri by his father.

I am also very grateful to Dr. Peter J. Brand, Professor of Egyptology at the University of Memphis, and Dr. Alice Stevenson, Curator of the Petrie Museum of Egyptian Archaeology, University College London, for their help in preparing this book.

— Katy Beebe

ILLUSTRATOR'S NOTE

One of the most fun parts of being an illustrator is imagining how the characters might appear. Although no one knows exactly what ancient Egyptians looked like, especially people from ordinary families like Khepri's, there are many artifacts that depict and describe people who lived during that time—ancient vessels, hieroglyphs on walls, and papyrus manuscripts. In addition to referencing books about these artifacts and archaeological excavations of this era, we also consulted historians for advice on how to illustrate the appearance of the characters and their surroundings as plausibly as we could. Even still, when depicting an ancient civilization, some amount of imagination must be used to bring the story to life.

I also looked at photographs of modern-day Egypt to understand the light and atmosphere in that part of the world. Movies and photos of Egypt show the same scenes that Katy's words describe—the bright sun and the strong desert shadows, the golden reflections on the shallow green water of the Nile River. I took inspiration from decorative textiles and patterns found in Egyptian art throughout history to create the borders for the book. And the line drawings are made to look like the black and reddish ink that the scribes would have used in their craft.

Many resources go into creating just one picture so that readers can feel and imagine that they are in the same setting and time as the characters they are reading about!

— Sally Wern Comport

GLOSSARY

AMULET—An object, often small enough to wear, which was thought to have the power to protect the owner from evil.

HIEROGLYPH—From the Greek meaning "sacred carving" or "sacred sign," a hieroglyph was a stylized picture that represented a sound, a syllable, or a word in the language of the ancient Egyptians. Hieroglyphs, a writing system in which these pictures conveyed meaning and language, was used in ancient Egypt from c. 4000 BCE to c. 400 CE.

KHEPRI—A form of the sun-god Re, who was depicted as a scarab. Khepri represented Re in his form as the morning sun. See also *Re/Ra* and *scarab*.

OSTRACON, OSTRACA (plural)—A broken piece of pottery that was used in ancient Egypt as a surface for writing, in the same way we might use sticky notes or notebook paper.

PAPYRUS—A type of reed-like plant that grows well in marshy conditions. Its triangular-shaped stem could be as tall as ten feet high. Since at least 3000 BCE, Ancient Egyptians split the papyrus stem and cut the pith inside into very thin strips, laid them crossways, hammered them, and then dried the finished sheet to create a paper-like surface for writing. A "papyrus" can also mean a document written on this material.

RE / RA—The high, creator god, who as Re or Ra, took the form of the sun. See also *Khepri*.

REED / RUSH—Plants that grow in or near water and have tall stems that are pithy or hollow inside. A single stem cut six to ten inches long could be used as a pen. See also *papyrus*.

SCARAB—A dung beetle sacred to the ancient Egyptians. Just as a scarab (*kheper* in their language) rolled balls of dung across the earth, the Egyptians thought that the sun god Re took the form of a scarab (as Khepri) to roll the ball of the sun across the sky each day. The verb *kheper* means "to create" or "to come into being."

SCRIBE—A person whose job was to write and keep records. Many school texts praised the profession of the scribe over all others.

SOBEK—The god of the Nile River, who took the form of a crocodile.

TAUERET / TAWERET—The goddess of childbirth, who took the form of a hippopotamus. She protected mothers and babies from evil spirits during childbirth.

THEBES—An important city on the bank of the Nile and capital of Upper Egypt. Townspeople lived on the eastern bank of the river. The red desert of the western side, beyond the narrow green band where Khepri and his family lived, was the city of the dead, where pharaohs built their tombs, and later rulers in the New Kingdom hid their graves in the Valley of the Kings.

THOTH—The god of wisdom, writing, and the moon, who was depicted with the head of an ibis or a baboon. Thoth is credited with inventing writing and hieroglyphs. He was the protector and patron of scribes.